Dogs at Work

Nicolas Brasch

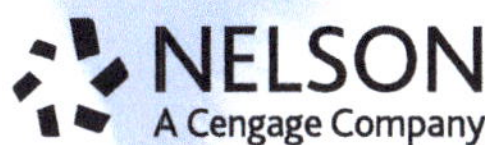

Australia • Brazil • Japan • Korea • Mexico • Singapore • Spain • United Kingdom • United States

Dogs at Work

Fast Forward
Emerald Level 25

Text: Nicolas Brasch
Editor: Cameron Macintosh
Design: Ami Sharpe
Series design: James Lowe
Production controller: Seona Galbally
Photo research: Michelle Cottrill
Audio recordings: Juliet Hill, Picture Start
Spoken by: Matthew King and Abbe Holmes
Reprint: Jennifer Foo

Acknowledgements
The author and publisher would like to acknowledge permission to reproduce material from the following sources: Photographs by AAP Image/ Andrew Brownbill, p 14/ Misha Japaridze, front cover top, pp 1 top, 23; Assistance Dogs Australia, front cover bottom, back cover, pp 1 bottom, 3, 4 left, 16, 18, 19; Getty Images, pp. 11, 21/ Alex Wong, p 20/ Erik S. Lesser, p 17/ Peter McBride, p 15/ Justin Sullivan, p 22; Istockphoto/ Sue McDonald, p 12; Newsphotos/ Kris Reichl, pp 8, 9/ Robert Pozo, p 7/ Stuart McEvoy, p 10/ Nicholas Wrankmore, p 13; Newspix/ Campbell Brodie, p 5; Photolibrary/ Lynn Stone, p 6; Photos.com, p 4 right.

ISBN 978 0 17 012723 3
ISBN 978 0 17 012717 2 (set)

Cengage Learning Australia
Level 7, 80 Dorcas Street
South Melbourne, Victoria Australia 3205
Phone: 1300 790 853

Cengage Learning New Zealand
Unit 4B Rosedale Office Park
331 Rosedale Road, Albany, North Shore NZ 0632
Phone: 0800 449 725

For learning solutions, visit **cengage.com.au**

Printed in Australia by Ligare Pty Limited
6 7 8 9 10 11 12 23 22 21 20 19

THE UNIVERSITY OF MELBOURNE

Evaluated in independent research by staff from the Department of Language, Literacy and Arts Education at the University of Melbourne.

Dogs at Work

Nicolas Brasch

Contents

Chapter 1	**Dogs Help People**	4
Chapter 2	**Guide Dogs**	6
Chapter 3	**Hospital Dogs**	10
Chapter 4	**Dogs as Carers**	14
Chapter 5	**Sniffer Dogs**	20
Glossary and Index		24

Chapter 1

DOGS HELP PEOPLE

Dogs are often called 'people's best friends'. They make good pets because they are loyal, playful and intelligent. There are different breeds of dogs to suit different people. Some people like small dogs, while other people like large dogs. Some people like dogs with lots of energy, while other people like quiet dogs.

Dogs don't just make great pets. They help people in many different ways.

Dogs are used to:

- help people with sight problems to move around safely
- help make stays in hospital more enjoyable for people
- care for people with a disability
- stop drugs and other illegal goods from coming into a country.

Chapter 2

GUIDE DOGS

Guide dogs help people who have major sight problems to move around safely. They help these people become more **independent** and less reliant on other people.

The most common breeds of dogs that are used as guide dogs are Labradors and Golden Retrievers. This is because they are calm, loyal and intelligent.

It takes about two years to train a puppy to be a guide dog. Puppies are trained by guide dog organisations and by families who take the puppies into their homes.

Case Study

Angela lost her sight in a sporting accident when she was 13. She is now 23 and is a student at university. Her guide dog, Boris, is a Labrador. He is her companion day and night.

Running Words 224

Although Angela is able to find her way from home to university without Boris, he warns her of hazards such as road works, broken pavements and cars that are not going to stop at a red light. He does this by guiding her around hazards or by stopping suddenly at the side of the road, so Angela knows to stop as well.

Chapter 3

HOSPITAL DOGS

Hospital dogs are dogs that are companions for people who are in hospital or in homes for the elderly. These people don't always get visitors, or sometimes the visitors they do get can't come every day. The company of a dog gives these people something to look forward to.

Some hospital dogs live in the hospital or home, while others are taken there for regular visits. The dogs may form an attachment with a patient, or with two or three patients.

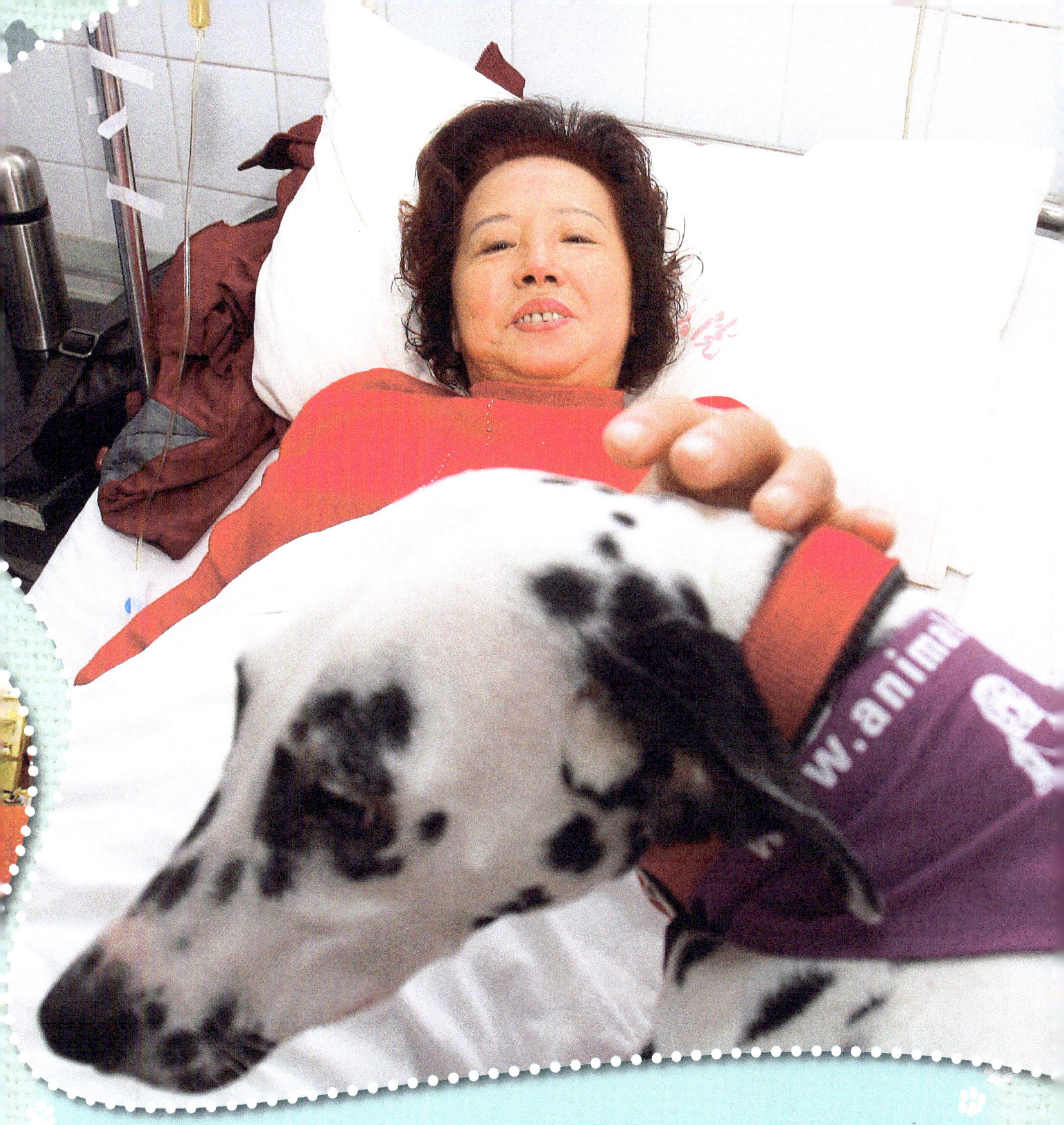

Many different types of dogs are trained as hospital dogs. They are given practice in an environment full of people and noises. The dogs that work best in this environment then start work as hospital dogs.

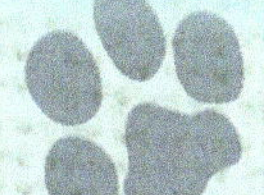
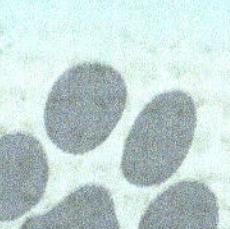

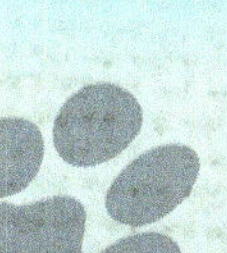

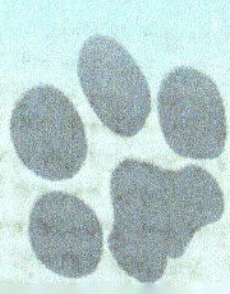
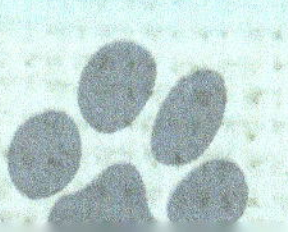

Case Study

Trudy is a King Charles Spaniel, and she is a hospital dog. She is a companion to Elsie, who lives in a home for the elderly. Trudy also lives in the home. Elsie is nearly 90 years old and will live in this home for the rest of her life.

Elsie's family visit her once a week, but Trudy provides her with company 24 hours a day. When Elsie is taken outside to enjoy the view and the open air, Trudy goes with her and runs around on the lawn. Without Trudy, Elsie would not be as happy and content as she is.

Chapter 4

DOGS AS CARERS

Some people have an illness or injury that affects the use of their hands, arms, legs or back. Or they might have very low energy levels, which means that they can't move very far. This means they cannot do some tasks, like opening doors or switching off lights. Sometimes, people with these conditions are given a dog to help care for them.

These dogs are trained to carry out simple but important tasks such as opening doors, turning lights on and off, picking up the telephone when it rings and pushing the wheelchair of the person they are helping to care for.

Labradors and Golden Retrievers are the most popular breeds of dogs to work as carers. This is because they have the right **temperament** – they are easy to train, loyal and reliable.

Dogs that work as carers are trained when they are puppies, and are taught more than 80 different commands.

Case Study

This is Brian. He has cerebral palsy, a condition that affects part of a person's brain and makes parts of their body difficult to move. Even though Brian has cerebral palsy, he still wants to live an independent life, so he lives in a flat with his Golden Retriever, Sunshine.

Sunshine was trained for more than a year, and then given to Brian for two weeks to make sure that they got along. They got along together from the very beginning and are now best friends.

Brian has trouble carrying objects, so Sunshine carries objects for him. One time, Brian fell and injured himself, and Sunshine pushed the emergency button that rang at the local hospital. Within 20 minutes, Brian was being helped by a doctor.

Chapter 5

SNIFFER DOGS

Sniffer dogs are trained to detect certain smells. Most sniffer dogs are used to detect illegal drugs, explosives or other dangerous devices. Some sniffer dogs are used at airports or at shipping ports where people try to smuggle drugs into a country. Other sniffer dogs are used by police in places where the police believe illegal drugs may be being used. These places include nightclubs, rock concerts and even some schools.

The most popular breeds that are used as sniffer dogs include Labradors and German Shepherds, because they have a very sharp sense of smell.

Case Study

Alby is a sniffer dog. He is a German Shepherd. Alby has been trained to sniff out explosives and other dangerous devices. He is used by the police to try to stop terrorist attacks. Alby is used in all sorts of places where a terrorist attack may be planned. If a suspicious package or bag is left at a train station, Alby sniffs the package or bag to see if he can detect an explosive device.

He is also used at airports to sniff baggage. Alby plays a major part in protecting people from terrorist attacks.

Glossary

independent able to look after oneself

temperament a person or animal's particular nature or character

Index

cerebral palsy 18

German Shepherds 21, 22

Golden Retrievers 6, 16, 18

guide dogs 6–9

hospital dogs 10–13

King Charles Spaniel 12

Labradors 6, 8, 16, 21

pets 4, 5

sniffer dogs 20–23